First published in the United States, Great Britain, Canada, Australia, and New Zealand in 2010
by North-South Books Inc., an imprint of NordSüd Verlag AG, CH-8005 Zürich, Switzerland.
Distributed in the United States by North-South Books Inc., New York 10001.

Library of Congress Cataloging-in-Publication Data is available.
ISBN: 978-0-7358-2291-7 (trade edition)
Printed in Belgium by Proost N.V., B 2300 Turnhout, November 2009.
1   3   5   7   9 • 10   8   6   4   2

www.northsouth.com

FSC
Mixed Sources
Product group from well-managed
forests and other controlled sources

Cert no. BV-COC-070303
www.fsc.org
© 1996 Forest Stewardship Council

Kristina Andres

Elephant in the Bathtub

NorthSouth
New York / London

One day Elephant filled
the bathtub with water and got in.

There was still plenty of room,
so Cat climbed in too.
He brought his box of tub toys.

Watch out,
Ducky!

There was still plenty of room,
so Baby Giraffe dropped in.

OOPS!

Then the mice joined the crew.

Next came Bear
with his water toy.

Then Alligator with his helicopter and
Rabbit pulling something big.
Cow biked in with a few friends.
Wait for us!
Where are we going?

We're going fishing on the high seas!

We already have a bite!

What a catch!
Reel it in!

What a strange fish.
It smells like a banana.

It's Ducky!

Now the crew is complete.

Everyone is ready to set sail for the high seas.

But what happened to the water?